Paula lives in a red brick house with a bright yellow door.

The bright yellow door was always open for friends to come in and play.

Paula was especially happy when her best friend Ben came to play.

Paula didn't see Ben in a while.
Where was Ben? Paula went outside
and saw him at the window of his house.
"I can't play with you, Paula. My daddy
says we need to stay home so that granny
won't get sick."

Paula had other friends to play with, but she missed Ben.

The next day, Mommy closed the bright yellow door. "I'm sorry, Paula. We have a pandemic. A pandemic means that many people are sick and many more will get sick. You can't play with your friends for a little while. If we all stay home, less people will get sick."

Daddy started working from home,
but he couldn't play with Paula.
Mommy looked worried.

Paula was sad. She felt alone.
She missed her friends.
She missed her school teacher.
She missed the big blue slide in the park.
And most of all, she missed Ben.

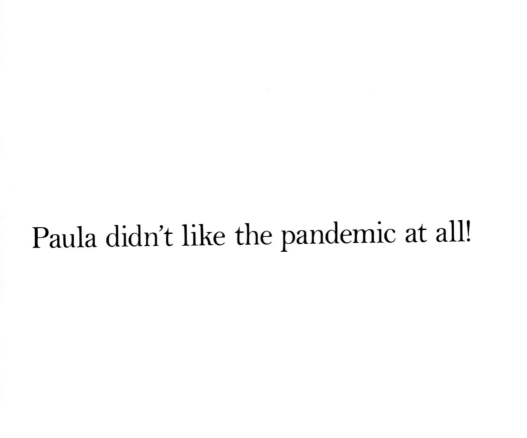

Paula didn't like the pandemic at all!

Then one morning, Mommy gave Paula a tiny seed.

Together, they dug a hole in the backyard and put the seed inside. Then they covered it with soil.
"We need to take good care of our seed," said Mommy.

"First, it will seem like the plant will never grow. But if we are patient, and water it and protect it from weeds, it will grow to be a big strong plant!"

"It's the same with the pandemic. It will take a long time, and we'll think that it will never be over and we'll never be able to play with our friends. But if we take good care of ourselves, and keep waiting, our community will grow back big and strong."

Paula liked watering her seed.

It seemed like nothing was happening for a long time. But then, one day...

... she saw a little sprout with one big green leaf!

Paula smiled. "Hello, little plant!"

Paula is not alone.
In all these houses are children
waiting for the end of the pandemic.
And if we are all patient, it will be
over before we know it!

For Helena and Johanna.

Hang in there, everyone!

Made in the USA
Middletown, DE
12 July 2020